Horace and Hattie are the very best of friends.

There are so many things they like to do together.

Hedgehugs

Autumn
Hide-and-Squeak

Steve Wilson & Lucy Tapper

GODWINBOOKS

Henry Holt and Company

NEW YORK

Henry Holt and Company, *Publishers since 1866*
Henry Holt® is a registered trademark of Macmillan Publishing Group, LLC.
175 Fifth Avenue, New York, New York 10010
mackids.com

Library of Congress Cataloging-in-Publication Data is available.
ISBN 978-1-250-11248-4

Our books may be purchased in bulk for promotional, educational, or business use.
Please contact your local bookseller or the Macmillan Corporate and Premium Sales Department
at (800) 221-7945 ext. 5442 or by e-mail at MacmillanSpecialMarkets@macmillan.com.

First published in the United Kingdom in 2016 by Maverick Arts Publishing Ltd.
First American edition—2017
Printed in China by RR Donnelley Asia Printing Solutions Ltd., Dongguan City, Guangdong Province

1 3 5 7 9 10 8 6 4 2

... and the tree came alive with colorful leaves, laughter, and lots of new squeaky friends!

Horace had an idea. He whispered
to their new little friend . . .

When the last leaf fell from the tree,
it was time for the squeaky thing to
return to his family. Hattie felt sad again.

The other two squealed in fright and delight.

SURPRISE!

Horace popped out of a pumpkin.

They looked and looked.

Horace waited and waited until . . .

Hattie hunted.

The squeaky thing searched.

The three friends giggled.

It was so much fun to play hide-and-squeak!

Horace had one last hiding place—

he'd spied a secret spot. . . .

Squeak! At last, they found him!

Horace and Hattie knew the squeaky thing was hidden somewhere beneath the toadstools and mushrooms.

among the seedpods.

It took the squeaky thing a long time to spot his friends

When they found him hidden in a tangle of brambles, he squeaked with joy.

. . . and seeking.

First Horace and Hattie searched for their new friend in the blackberry bushes.

They were experts at hiding . . .

Horace and Hattie loved
to play games too.

The squeaky thing thought it was a game—he loved to play hide-and-seek!

Horace and Hattie leaped with surprise.

They landed in a pile of leaves.

something squeaked!

Horace didn't want Hattie to be sad. He gathered up as many leaves as he could and was trying to put them back on the tree when suddenly . . .

One windy autumn day, the sky was filled with leaves falling from the trees. It was pretty, but Hattie felt sad that the branches would soon be empty.

When Horace is busy, Hattie likes
to decorate her nest.

When Hattie is busy,
Horace likes to
practice his music.

And after a rain, they like to
spot sparkling spiderwebs.

and catch dewdrops from leaves.

They like to follow shiny snail trails

They like to make funny shadows as the sun comes up.